Unveiling Beauty - Odes to the Extraordinary

A Celestial Reverie

Hrishikesh Goswami

ISBN 978-93-5667-778-4
© Hrishikesh Goswami 2023

Published in India 2023 by Pencil

A brand of
One Point Six Technologies Pvt. Ltd.
Unit no. 26, Ground Floor, Building A1,
Wadala Truck Terminal Road,
Near Post Office, Antop Hill, Mumbai - 400037
E connect@thepencilapp.com
W www.thepencilapp.com

DISCLAIMER: *The opinions expressed in this book are those of the authors and do not purport to reflect the views of the Publisher.*

Author biography

(India Book of Records Holder)

(Creative Endeavour of The Month April 2021 by The Assam Tribune)

(Recipient of India Prime Top 100 Author Award 2022)

(Recipient of India Star Icon Award 2022)

(Author of The Year 2021 Nominee)

(Recipient of The Leading Attainers Award 2022)

HRISHIKESH GOSWAMI is a Contemporary Naturalistic poet from Assam, India who specialises in writing about nature and realism coalescing fiction and non-fiction in a sophisticated blend.

Author of The Poet's Words, The Secret: Nature Reveals, Poems for Poets, The Exegesis, 72 Haiku, 51st Tanka, The Sesquipedalian Notion, An Aureate Opus of Quotes, An Ode To, The Arcane: The Adventures in Lavender, The Arcane: The Ultimate Fate, A Poet's Whim For Serendipity, A Fortuitous Odyssey, The Adventures of James Tony Morgan along with Co-Author of World Record Anthology Book – "Bilingual Aesthetics" and editor of the E-Poetry Anthology 'The Euphoric Verses from Soul' and the Literary Anthology 'Forest & Me' and 'The Idiosyncratic Mystery'.

Hrishikesh Goswami fell in love with writing from a fledgling age of 14 when he was at the 9th standard. Hrishikesh Goswami's poems have been featured in The Assam Tribune, Blue Lake Review, Indian Poetry Review, the Weaver Magazine, Poets India, Soul Connection brought up by Guwahati Grand Poetry Festival, Anthology Still I Rise brought out by Wingless Dreamer, Winter Poems Anthology brought out by Poets Choice.

Hrishikesh Goswami has been highlighted by Media Houses such as India Saga, Daily hunt, Spot Latest, Fox Story India, Glamwist etc. Hrishikesh Goswami is also available in E platforms like Story mirror, Anchor, Spotify, Wattpad, Google Podcast, Apple Podcast, Breaker, Pocket Cast, Radio Public, All Poetry, Listen Notes, Wynk Music, Poetry Soup, Commaful, Hello Poetry, SoundCloud, Poem

Hunter, Scribd, Vivlio, Angus & Robertson Store, Mondadori Store, Thalia, Indigo Books & Music, Kobo Inc., Apple Books etc. for his dear readers. Readers can find further information about the poet in Google and YouTube by typing "POET HRISHIKESH GOSWAMI " for the same.

Hrishikesh Goswami has cracked several competitive exams such as JEE Mains 2022, NEET-UG 2022, CUET 2022, IISER IAT 2022, KVPY 2022, AAU CET 2022, ASTU CEE 2022, IOQB-I and IOQC-I.

He has been bestowed with Certificate of Commendation in Never Such Innocence International Poetry Contest, Certificate of Achievement from Asian Council for English Proficiency Test conducted under CAFLR norms, Certificate of Merit for Outstanding Performance in NationWide Mega Science Experiment Conducted by NCERT, VVM, VIBHA and Ministry of Education, Govt. of India, Editor's Choice Award in International Essay Writing Competition by Monomousumi and is recognised by World Record University, Career Development College London, Guwahati Grand Poetry Festival, WWF India, APJ. Abdul Kalam International Foundation, ASSIST WORLD RECORDS, PONDICHERRY BOOK OF RECORDS and Royal Commonwealth Society.

He has been two times State Level Tae-kwon-do Champion, Gold Medallist of several National and International Competitive Exams and Olympiads, a KVPY Scholar, Winner of National School Level Essay Writing Contest conducted by Maulana Abul Kalam Azad Awards 2020, Grand Master of Mental Arithmetic-Senior A Whole

Brain Development Program from Aloha (Abacus), Visharat in Hindustani Classical Music, Best Debater of PRARAMBH 2021 conducted by Nehru Group of Institutions, Kerala and Holder of Honourable Mention in several notable Poetry Competitions from around the World.

Apart from these Hrishikesh's poems have been critically analysed by Fruit Journal Manchester (UK), Acorn (A journal of contemporary haiku), The Leading Edge Magazine, BreakBread Magazine and has been published by The Assam Tribune's Horizon and Planet Young, NEZINE (An online magazine), Noverse Foundation and FoxGales Publishers, Poem hunter-The World's Poetry Archive, Cultural Reverence (An International Digital Journal Of Art and Literature), Tech Touch Talk of Kolkata.

Hrishikesh Goswami's poems have been read by The Liminal Review, Poetry London, Appalachian Review, The Tether's End, Tears in the Fence Literary Journal, MASKS Literary Magazine, Ribbons, The Hopper (An environmental literary magazine), The West Trade Review, Split Rock Review, The Baltimore Review, Rollick Magazine, The Poetry Magazine, Chestnut Review, The Sun Magazine, The Society of Classical Poets, The Greensboro Review, The London Magazine, The Kenyon Review, The Adroit Journal, Washington Square Review, Wilderness House Literary Review and many more.

Hrishikesh's haiku poem has been translated into Japanese and published in a traditional Japanese style literary anthology.

CONTENTS

Preface

My journey of Ode writing started somewhere years ago which I today fail to recall. Nevertheless my journey was adventurous, full of ups and downs, filled with evanescent moments of joy and sorrow which then receded along with the retroceding sea. My journey also taught me several treasured lessons which I would like to share with the mass.

Firstly, never give up. Be it your hope, dreams or desire to achieve something worthy. The joy of achieving it needs no explanation. Secondly, work as hard as you possibly can. Hard Work surely repays as it has a high credibility. Last but not the least, always try to learn from your silly as well as grave mistakes as they will aid you in your journey of becoming a perfect human (if possible).

Acknowledgements

I find immense pleasure in appreciating the ones who have passionately contributed either openly or meanderingly to this manuscript. I am profoundly thankful to all those who have reinforced me through the construction of this book. Firstly, I would like to thank my family for their steadfast affection and backing. Their belief in my capabilities has been a relentless source of motivation. I also want to express my gratitude to my friends who have been my sounding board, offering their insights and criticism to help polish my work.

I am also indebted to the publishing team for their hard work and commitment in bringing this project to fruition.

Lastly, I want to thank the readers of this book, whose interest and support make all the effort worthwhile. It is my hope that these odes will inspire you to find delight and miracle in the world around you. The sole purpose of this book is to rejuvenate your mind by reflecting on nature's self-generated creations!

Introduction

In this collection of odes that I have prepared vehemently, we embark on an expedition through the beauty of the ugly, the ordinary or the marvellous. With words as our escort, we reconnoitre the depths of the soul, finding bliss and marvel in the mundane.

Each ode is a celebration, a tribute to the occult matter that surrounds us all. From the chirping of birds to the balminess of the sun, from the scent of renewed rain to the flavour of a perfect cup of coffee, we revel in the sensual experiences that make life worth living. So join me, dear reader, as we push into the grandeur of existence, one ode at a time.

Ode to Fire

(Published by Poetsindia.com)

The birth of whose is known
Unlike its death
The sound of whose
Is quite familiar
To dramatic ears
The smell of whose
Is nostalgic
And the colour
Of whose is brilliant
One that warms me up
And my soul
One that cooks the food
They eat
And one that burns down
The refuse
Sometimes
Burns down the colossal Amazon
Sometimes
Takes away the soul
Sometimes
Dresses up in an unfamiliar attire.

Don't orphan us
You are our beloved fire.

Anti-Ode to Summer

When the Sun sheens
Stout and Solid
Over the dancing tall swards
It scorches them down
To ashes
It kills the microbes
Latent in the summer soil
And dries
The autumn parched leaves!

Summer is heartless
Merciless
Much alike a butcherer
Who sees return
In the plasma of the extra cadaver
He slaughters
He needs them for persistence
They need them for pleasure
For nature decides always
Who stands and who falls!
Just like the wilting flower
Of the summer seared plant!

Ode to Literature

(Published by Guwahati Grand Poetry Festival)

Who on this planet
Has never ever read
A text
Which passes straight
Through the human heart?

Literature is very very vast
Vaster than you have imagined!
What you can do
Is grab one end and linger
But we often don't ponder
The life devoid of literature
It will be a soul without palate
Or an ode without any manuscript!

Literature delineates life
It delimits relationships
It defines nature
So does it
Defines us

Universe is tasteless
Without it

Flowers are mere accumulation of atoms and molecules
Without the nectar of literature!

Ode to Time

(Published by Guwahati Grand Poetry Festival)

I see you everyday
Passing by the stand
But fail to halt you
Even for a cup of coffee
You are too busy
For me to comprehend you.

You need to reach your ultimate goal which is not
demarcated
For me
For we only see you, feel you but cannot understand you
Then you say…
How do I…
How do I write an Ode to you?!
Even the ode will be imperfect
Without sparing you!

Ode to Spring

(Published in January-March, 2022 issue of Soul Connection by Guwahati Grand Poetry Festival.)

How alluring is the spring...!
Do you remember your antecedent
Encounter with the Spring?
Perhaps you don't!

Spring is indeed propitious
It is the penillion of Nature
It speaks only of subtle upholster
And that is what
Makes it so voguish
Among the thinkers
And its lovers.

Spring fetches with itself
New longing
And inducement
To recreate
Our psyche
Which was shuttered by
The combined forces
Of Autumn and Winter

Proclivity, is what comes to mind
When thee prattle of Spring (2)

Without thee,
Life will be colourless, remorseless
Tawdry and vicious
Time will run frenzied
And poems will clash
With each other!!

Ode to the Rain

You may love monsoon
And so do I…
You may love after rains
And so do I…

But what if it rains too plenty
Or what if it rains too less
We will grieve
Suffer losses like never before
We wilt our time
Thinking about the rain

But is that wilt the case
Rain gives me hope
It brings me desires
To achieve something impossible otherwise!

Rain brings wisdom
It cherishes joy
It lugs mirth and yell
All together…

Ode to Beauty

Beauty is what is invisible.
Beauty is somewhat mystic.
Beauty has possessions distinct from else
It has the command to change
The state of mind
Or the state of the soul

What defines Beauty…
Is ether
What defines its ode…
Is void

Then how can I explain
The presence or absence
Of beauty anywhere?

Ode to Generosity

How can I help you
Comprehend the beauty of
Generosity?!

Generosity is gorgeous, it is something that presents
The superiority of the soul
And liberal nature of the mind

It builds bonds
It builds happiness
Both in the minds of the
Giver and heritor
It reduces the emotional gaps
Between them
And make them feel connected.

To envisage a world
Without generosity
Might be very laidback for you
But not for me
For I felt it
Very very abysmal
In my veins
In my own physique!

An Ode to Food

(Published as 'Bliss on a Plate' by Guwahati Grand Poetry
Festival)

Food is what we
All want to palate
It feels certainly relishing
When we get a bit to
Chomp upon

Food rejuvenates us
And permits us to
Attain what we desire
Or what we be worthy of

A day in the truancy of food
Is not what many would adore
For each day our body is getting
Rebuild with what we eat!

An Ode to Flowers

How appealing they look,
The flowers
Pirouetting along the waft

I just love
To devote my time
Observing the jovial bees
Slurping nectar
From those flowers
For these flowers give rise to fruits
Which in turn nourishes us.

Flowers give us aesthetic inclination
And fervently strengthens us
To fight the worst of all situations.

Flowers teaches us to be
Eye-catching
Not superficially but from within!

This world would be pallid
Without flowers blooming
All around the green globe!

An Ode to Leaf

The thin green leaf,
Garnishes the stout tree
As if it has given her
Shelter for
The most challenging night.

The leaf gives us aesthetic pleasure
And plethora of inestimable stuff
Such as nutrition, oxygen and linctus
It revitalises our hassled minds
And freshens our breathes
It adds aroma to our food
And taste to our lives.

It performs several vibrant functions
Whose price can never be paid
By humankind.

An Ode to Parents

You are the greatest of all.
Your presence in itself
Is a matter of infinite joy
In the soft cores
Of the timid creatures
You nourish us
Teach us to act
In accordance to society
You make us true human
You work tirelessly for us
We can't repay the entire debt
But yes, we can do one thing!
We can dedicate our entire life
In your service.

An Ode to Mother Earth

A mother knows
The agony of her kids
She apprehends them far better
Than anyone else
This mother also shelters
Everyone and everybody
She has a limitless heart for all.
She permits us to harm her
Only for our own profit
She is none other than
Our beloved Mother Earth.

Appendix

OTHER BOOKS FROM THE POET

Notes

Further Reading

HOW TO BALANCE
COACHING WITH
SCHOOL?
HRISHIKESH GOSWAMI

THE
ARCANE
THE ADVENTURES
IN LAVENDER
HRISHIKESH
GOSWAMI

HOW TO
CRACK
NEET-UG?
Everything
you need to
know!
FIRST
EDITION
HRISHIKESH GOSWAMI

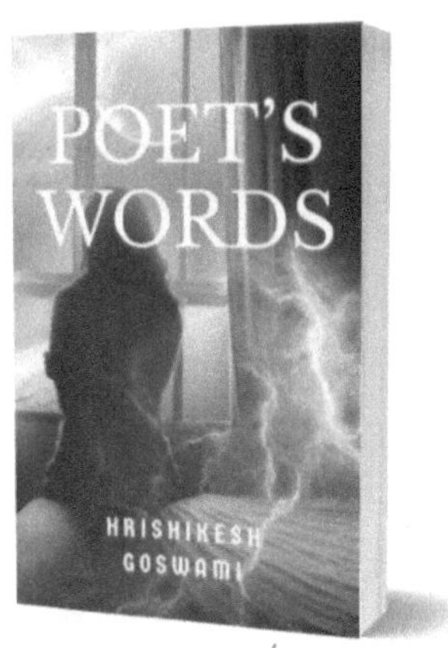

POET'S
WORDS
HRISHIKESH
GOSWAMI

AN
AUREATE
OPUS OF QUOTES
HRISHIKESH GOSWAMI

THE
SESQUIPEDALIAN
NOTION
Adventure of Long
Lost Humanity
HRISHIKESH GOSWAMI

POEMS
FOR
POETS
HRISHIKESH GOSWAMI

THE
SECRET:
NATURE REVEALS
A COLLECTION OF PURELY EXPRESSED
HEART FEELINGS AND VEHEMENCE
HRISHIKESH
GOSWAMI

THE EXEGESIS
HRISHIKESH
GOSWAMI

72
HAIKU
HRISHIKESH
GOSWAMI